Beyond DNA: The Epigenetic Revolution

"From Cellular Mechanisms to Environmental Factors: How Epigenetics Shapes Our Biological Destiny and its Implications for Health, Behavior, and the Future of Research"

Narrated Molecules

1. Introduction to Epigenetics
- Definition and Origin of the Term
- Distinguishing Genetics from Epigenetics

2. Biological Foundations of Epigenetics
- The Role of DNA
- Chromatids and Their Interaction with Genes

3. Major Epigenetic Mechanisms
- DNA Methylation
- Histone Modifications
- Non-coding RNA and Its Epigenetic Functions

4. Epigenetics and Human Development
- Epigenetic Guidance from Embryo to Adulthood
- Cellular Differentiation and Specialization

5. Environmental Factors and Epigenetics
- Environmental Influence on Epigenetic Changes

- Examples: Diet, Stress, Pollution

6. Epigenetics and Diseases
- Epigenetic Involvement in Disease Causation or Contribution
- Current Epigenetic Research on Diseases like Cancer

7. Epigenetics and Behavior
- Twin Studies' Insights into Epigenetics and Personality
- The Influence of Epigenetics on Choices and Behaviors

8. Epigenetic Manipulation and Its Implications
- Potential for "Editing" Epigenetic Modifications
- Ethical Considerations and Associated Risks

9. Case Studies and Recent Research
- Spotlight on Notable Epigenetic Research

- The Latest Scientific Findings in Epigenetics

10. Conclusion and the Future of Epigenetics
- Current State and Future Prospects in Epigenetic Research

Introduction to Epigenetics

Definition and Origin of the Term:
Epigenetics, from the Greek "epi-" (above, over) and "genetics," concerns genome modifications that do not alter the DNA nucleotide sequence but influence gene expression. It is a field of study that investigates heritable changes in gene function that do not involve a change in DNA sequence. These modifications are "above" the genome and regulate which genes are expressed, when, and to what extent. The term "epigenetics" was first coined by 20th-century biologist C. H. Waddington, who used it to describe interactions between genes and the developmental pathways of organisms. Initially, epigenetics was associated with the

concept of how genes interact with their environment to produce a phenotype. Only more recently, with discoveries about chemical modifications of DNA and DNA-associated proteins like histones, has the field of epigenetics expanded to include these molecular modifications.

Distinction Between Genetics and Epigenetics: Genetics involves the study of genes, their heredity, and functions. It focuses on the DNA nucleotide sequence, which is the fundamental "recipe" for building and maintaining an organism. When mutations or changes occur in this sequence, genetic diseases or variations among individuals may emerge. Epigenetics, on the other hand, deals with modifications that do not change the DNA sequence but still influence gene expression. For example, a gene can be "switched on" or "off" due to an epigenetic signal, thus influencing whether a particular protein is produced by a cell. These epigenetic modifications are crucial for various processes, such as embryonic development and cell differentiation, and can be influenced by a range of factors, including environmental ones. A simple way to understand the difference is to think of a book: genetics is like the words in a book, while epigenetics is like the punctuation. Even though the words (the genetic sequence) remain the same, punctuation (epigenetic modifications) can change the meaning of a sentence or determine which words are read aloud.

Continuation of the Book: In the continuation of this book, we will explore various types of epigenetic modifications, how they are formed, how they influence gene expression, and their impact on health and disease. This introduction serves as a starting point for understanding the importance and complexity of epigenetic regulation in the broader biological context.

Biological Fundamentals of Epigenetics

DNA and Its Role: DNA, or deoxyribonucleic acid, is the fundamental hereditary molecule in all known forms of life. It is found in the nucleus of every cell and contains the genetic instructions used in the development and functioning of all living organisms. The structure of DNA consists of two strands twisted together to form a double helix. Each strand is a sequence of nucleotides, each composed of a sugar (deoxyribose), a phosphate group, and a nitrogenous base. There are four nitrogenous bases in DNA: adenine (A), thymine (T), cytosine (C), and guanine (G). The specific sequence of these bases determines genetic information; for example, a sequence might indicate the construction of a particular protein. DNA serves as a template during the transcription process, where it is copied into RNA, and subsequently, RNA is translated into proteins during the translation process. These proteins perform vital functions inside the cell and the organism.

What Are Chromatids and How Do They Relate to Genes? Chromatids are replicated units of DNA, meaning two identical copies of DNA bound together at a point called the centromere. During cell division, chromatids separate and move into different daughter cells. Each chromatid contains a copy of the organism's genome. In mammals, DNA is organized into complex structures called chromosomes. A chromosome consists of a long DNA molecule wound around specialized proteins called histones. This compact structure allows DNA to fit inside the cell nucleus. Humans have 23 pairs of chromosomes, for a total of 46. Each chromosome contains many genes, which are specific segments of DNA containing instructions to produce specific proteins. Epigenetics comes into play in how genes on chromosomes are expressed or repressed. Even though all cells in an organism have the same DNA, not all cells express the same genes. This is why a skin cell is different from a liver cell or a brain cell, despite all of them containing the same DNA. Epigenetic modifications determine which genes are "switched on" or "off" in a particular cell or at a particular moment.

With a solid foundation on DNA's structure, function, and how it is organized within cells, we can now begin to explore how epigenetics influences this organization and function by regulating gene expression without altering the underlying DNA sequence.

Histone Proteins and Chromatin: DNA, although a long and complex molecule, must fit within the confined space of the cell nucleus. This is made possible through its interaction with proteins known as histones. This combination of DNA and histones is referred to as chromatin. Histones are globular proteins around which DNA wraps, forming structures called nucleosomes. Imagine a nucleosome as a "spool," and DNA as a "thread" wound around it. The sequence at which DNA wraps around histones can be modified by epigenetic signals, which, in turn, influence DNA's accessibility to proteins that regulate transcription and, therefore, gene expression.

DNA Compaction and Gene Accessibility

Chromatin can exist in a "relaxed" state (euchromatin) or a "compact" state (heterochromatin). When relaxed, proteins that read DNA can easily access it, and genes in those regions can be transcribed into RNA. When compact, DNA access is limited, and transcription is inhibited. The transition between these two states is regulated by epigenetic modifications. For example, methylation of specific amino acid residues on histones can lead to chromatin compaction and gene repression, while other modifications can promote a relaxed chromatin state and gene activation.

The Interplay between DNA and RNA

While DNA's sequence encodes genetic information, RNA acts as a messenger, carrying this information from DNA to ribosomes where proteins are synthesized. However, not all RNA serves as a messenger. There are many varieties of non-coding RNA with diverse functions, some of which are involved in epigenetic regulation. For instance, certain types of small RNAs, such as siRNAs and miRNAs, can guide protein complexes to specific DNA regions, leading to gene repression. These mechanisms underscore the important interaction between DNA and RNA in the epigenetic context.

Cellular Environment and Epigenetics

The internal environment of a cell is not static. Variations such as oxidative stress, nutrient availability, or hormonal signals can influence the epigenetic landscape. For example, a deficiency in a key nutrient could alter the DNA methylation profile of the cell, thus affecting gene expression. These internal environmental factors highlight how epigenetics serves as an interface between the cell's environment and its genome, allowing the cell to dynamically respond to challenges and changes.

This in-depth exploration aimed to provide a more detailed overview of the biological foundations of epigenetics, emphasizing the central role of DNA, histone proteins, and molecular interactions within the cell. As we continue to explore epigenetics, we will see how these biological foundations give rise to

complex regulatory mechanisms that define gene expression.

Methylation Molecules and Their Role

One of the most studied epigenetic processes is DNA methylation. This involves adding a methyl group (CH_3) to one of the DNA nitrogenous bases, usually cytosine. Methylation typically has a repressive effect on gene expression. Methylation is not a random process. It is carried out by enzymes called DNA methyltransferases. These enzymes recognize specific sequences in DNA and add a methyl group at precise positions. The accumulation of methylation in particular genome regions, such as gene promoters, can prevent genes from being expressed.

Demethylation and Epigenetic Dynamics

Equally important as methylation is the reverse process, demethylation. This is the removal of methyl groups from DNA, potentially "switching on" gene expression. Enzymes involved in this process are known as DNA demethylases. The interplay of methylation and demethylation highlights that epigenetics is not static. Instead, it is a dynamic series of events that can change over an organism's lifetime or in response to environmental changes.

Histone Modifications and Post-Translational Changes

We have already discussed how histones help package DNA inside the nucleus. But histones themselves can undergo a range of post-translational chemical modifications, such as methylation, acetylation, phosphorylation, and ubiquitination. These modifications can influence chromatin structure and, consequently, DNA accessibility. Histone acetylation, for example, generally makes chromatin less compact and promotes gene expression. Conversely, deacetylation, carried out by enzymes called histone deacetylases, can repress gene expression.

Epigenetic Modifications and Diseases

Malfunctions in epigenetic mechanisms can lead to various issues, including diseases. For example, aberrant methylation of certain genes can lead to their inappropriate expression, which may contribute to cancer development. This has led to intensive research into the role of epigenetics in cancer, with the hope of developing epigenetic therapies as new treatment options.

Implications of Epigenetics in Future Research

With an increasing understanding of the importance of epigenetics in biology, it is becoming evident that we must consider not only the information encoded in DNA but also how this information is interpreted and modified in response to the environment. This opens up new frontiers in biomedical research, genetics, and personalized medicine.

Epigenetics represents one of the most exciting and rapidly evolving frontiers in modern science, and its study may revolutionize our understanding of many diseases and the molecular foundations of life itself.

Epigenetic Interaction and the Environment

One of the most fascinating areas of epigenetic research concerns how the external environment can influence epigenetic mechanisms. Factors such as diet, toxin exposure, stress, and even social experiences can affect DNA methylation and histone modifications. **Nutrition and Epigenetics:** It has been shown that a deficiency in certain nutrients during pregnancy can have epigenetic effects on the fetus that can last a lifetime. For example, inadequate intake of folic acid can lead to DNA methylation variations. **Stress and Epigenetic Response:** Trauma and prolonged stress can result in changes in the epigenetic profile. For instance, exposure to traumatic stress at a young age can lead to increased methylation levels in specific genes, which could contribute to susceptibility to mental illnesses in adulthood.

Epigenetic Therapies

Understanding the connection between epigenetics and disease has opened the door to the development of epigenetic therapies. These therapies aim to correct epigenetic abnormalities associated with diseases.

- **DNA Methyltransferase Inhibitors:** These drugs aim to block the action of enzymes responsible for adding methyl groups to DNA. They are particularly used in some cancer therapies.

- **Histone Deacetylase Inhibitors:** These drugs increase histone acetylation, facilitating the expression of genes that may be repressed in tumors.

Epigenetic Inheritance

There is growing evidence that some epigenetic modifications can be inherited across generations. If an individual undergoes epigenetic changes due to environmental exposure, these changes could be passed on to their descendants, even if the DNA undergoes no mutations.

Epigenomics: A New Frontier

With the increasing understanding of the importance of epigenetic processes, a new field of study has emerged: epigenomics. Epigenomics refers to the comprehensive analysis of epigenetic modification patterns across the entire genome. Through epigenomics, scientists hope to create detailed maps of how epigenetics influences gene activity in different conditions and stages of development.

Conclusion

While the genetic code provides the instructions for the development and functioning of an organism, epigenetics represents the sophisticated regulation that decides when, where, and how these instructions are executed. With its dynamic response to the environment and its ability to influence health across generations, epigenetics represents a crucial key to understanding not only biology but also the complex interactions between genes and the environment.

2. Epigenetic Mechanisms: An Overview

Fundamental Epigenetic Mechanisms

Epigenetic mechanisms are molecular processes that modify gene activity without altering the underlying DNA sequence. These modifications are reversible and influence how genes are read by cells, determining whether they are expressed or repressed.

DNA Methylation

- **What Is It?:** Methylation is the addition of a methyl group (CH_3) to a DNA base, typically cytosine. This process is catalyzed by enzymes called DNA methyltransferases.

- **Function:** Methylation, especially in gene promoter regions, tends to repress gene expression. Hypermethylation of the genome, in general, results in reduced gene expression.

- **Implications in Health:** Aberrant methylation can be associated with various pathologies, including cancers. In some diseases like tumors, altered methylation profiles can lead to the activation of oncogenes or the repression of tumor suppressor genes.

Histone Modifications

- **Introduction:** Histones are fundamental proteins around which DNA wraps, forming complexes called nucleosomes. These proteins can undergo various post-translational modifications.

- **Types of Modifications:** These include acetylation, methylation, phosphorylation, ubiquitination, and sumoylation. Each of these modifications can influence chromatin structure and its accessibility to transcription factors and, consequently, gene expression.

- **Enzymes Involved:** Histone modifications are catalyzed by various enzymes, such as histone acetyltransferases (HATs) that add acetyl groups and histone deacetylases (HDACs) that remove acetyl groups.

Non-Coding RNAs and Epigenetics

- **Definition:** Non-coding RNAs (ncRNAs) are RNA molecules that do not code for proteins. Instead, they regulate gene expression at various levels.

- **Epigenetic Role:** Some ncRNAs are involved in epigenetic processes. For example, Xist ncRNAs are involved in X chromosome inactivation in female mammals.

- **Implications:** ncRNAs are often dysregulated in various diseases, including cancers, where they can act as oncogenes or tumor suppressor genes.

Epigenetic Memory and Cellular Differentiation

- **Concept:** During development, cells differentiate into various cell types, each with a distinct gene expression profile. Epigenetic changes play a crucial role in maintaining these stably inherited profiles during cell divisions.

- **Stability and Flexibility:** While epigenetic modifications are stable and allow the cell to "remember" its state, they are also reversible, allowing flexibility and response to environmental changes.

Epigenetic mechanisms are fundamental for gene expression regulation. They provide cells with the flexibility to respond to environmental cues and maintain gene expression integrity during development and differentiation. Abnormalities in epigenetic mechanisms can lead to pathologies but also offer new therapeutic opportunities, as epigenetic modifications, unlike genetic mutations, are potentially reversible.

Modifications of Histones and Chromatin Structure Chromatin structure plays a central role in gene expression regulation. Chromatin can exist in a more relaxed state (euchromatin) that is accessible to the transcription machinery or in a more compact state (heterochromatin) generally associated with gene repression.

- **Histone Acetylation:** When histones are acetylated, typically on histone H3 and H4, chromatin adopts a relaxed conformation, allowing transcription activation. Histone acetyltransferases (HATs) are responsible for adding acetyl groups to histones, while histone deacetylases (HDACs) remove these groups.

- **Histone Methylation:** Unlike acetylation, methylation can have both activating and repressive effects on transcription, depending on the context and specific position. For example, methylation of lysine 4 on histone H3 (H3K4me) is associated with activation, whereas methylation of lysine 9 (H3K9me) is associated with repression.

Implications of DNA Methylation in Health and Disease DNA methylation is not a static process and can change in response to various environmental stimuli and during development. Improper regulation is implicated in several diseases.

- **Genomic Imprinting:** It's an epigenetic process through which only one of the two alleles of a gene is expressed, depending on whether the allele comes from the mother or the father. Aberrations in imprinting can lead to diseases such as Angelman syndrome or Prader-Willi syndrome.

- **Neurodegenerative Diseases:** Recent studies have shown that DNA methylation changes may play a role in diseases like Alzheimer's and Parkinson's.

Non-Coding RNAs and Epigenetic Function
While the importance of non-coding RNAs in epigenetics has only recently been recognized, these RNAs play crucial roles in chromatin structure regulation and gene expression.

- **siRNA and piRNA:** These small interfering RNAs are involved in heterochromatin formation and silencing of harmful transcripts, such as those from transposable elements.

- **lncRNA:** Long non-coding RNAs can interact with both DNA and proteins to form structures that regulate gene activity. For example, the previously mentioned Xist RNA is an lncRNA that plays a key role in X chromosome inactivation.

Epigenetic Mechanisms, though complex, offer extraordinary opportunities to understand how genes are regulated in response to the environment and during development. Abnormalities in these processes can lead to diseases, but the reversible nature of epigenetic changes also offers hope for new therapies. With increasing research in this field, we are likely to see new discoveries and medical applications in the coming years.

Epigenetic Therapy and Clinical Implications
With growing awareness of the importance of

epigenetic processes in gene expression regulation and their implications in disease, there is increasing interest in targeting these modifications for therapeutic purposes. Epigenetic alterations, unlike genetic mutations, are potentially reversible, making them an attractive target for treating various pathologies.

- **HDAC Inhibitors (Histone Deacetylase):** These compounds can increase histone acetylation, leading to the reactivation of suppressed genes. HDAC inhibitors are currently in clinical use for treating certain types of cancer, such as cutaneous T-cell lymphoma.

- **DNA Demethylating Agents:** Compounds like azacitidine and decitabine can reduce DNA methylation, potentially reactivating epigenetically silenced genes. These drugs are used in the treatment of some hematological diseases, such as myelodysplastic syndrome.

- **Targeting Non-Coding RNAs:** Non-coding RNAs, especially lncRNAs, are emerging as potential therapeutic targets due to their key roles in many cellular and pathological processes. Small molecules or antisense oligonucleotides could be used to modulate the function of these ncRNAs.

Epigenetics and the Environment The environment in which we live can have a significant impact on our epigenetic profile. Factors such as diet, stress, toxin exposure, and early-life experiences can influence DNA methylation and histone modifications.

- **Early Exposures and Long-Term Effects:** There is growing evidence that experiences during fetal development or early childhood, such as malnutrition or stress, can cause epigenetic changes with long-term health effects.

- **Epigenetics and Aging:** With advancing age, epigenetic changes can influence susceptibility to diseases and longevity. Some research suggests that interventions like caloric restriction could influence the epigenetic profile and potentially affect lifespan.

Epigenetic research is revealing new dimensions of how our genes function and how they are influenced by our environment. The therapeutic possibilities arising from this understanding are highly promising, especially considering the potential reversibility of epigenetic modifications. However, with this power comes great responsibility: fully understanding the long-term effects of such interventions and ensuring they are used ethically and effectively. The frontier of epigenetics promises to be an exciting and evolving area of biomedicine in the near future.

Major Epigenetic Mechanisms: An In-Depth Look Histone Modifications: Histones are fundamental globular proteins for the nucleosome's structure, the basic unit of chromatin. Each nucleosome consists of an octamer of histones around which DNA is wound. The amino-terminal tails of these histones protrude from the nucleosome and are the site of various post-translational modifications.

- **Histone Acetylation:** Acetylation of lysines in histone tails plays a crucial role in gene expression regulation. The presence of acetyl groups makes chromatin less compact, allowing transcriptional machinery to access DNA. This is often associated with highly transcribed DNA regions. The enzymes involved in this process, HATs and HDACs, are often targets of anticancer drugs due to their importance in gene expression regulation.

- **Histone Methylation:** Unlike acetylation, histone methylation can have both activating and repressive effects on gene expression. For example, trimethylation of lysine 27 on histone H3 (H3K27me3) is associated with gene repression, while trimethylation of lysine 4 on histone H3

(H3K4me3) is associated with gene activation.

- **Additional Modifications:** Histones can undergo various other modifications, including phosphorylation, ubiquitination, sumoylation, and ADP-ribosylation. Each of these modifications has unique effects on chromatin and gene transcription, and the combination of these modifications, often referred to as the "histone code," can have complex impacts on gene regulation.

Non-Coding RNA and Its Role in Epigenetics: The discovery of non-coding RNAs has revolutionized our understanding of gene regulation. Although they do not encode proteins, these RNAs have crucial functions in orchestrating gene expression.

- **MicroRNA (miRNA):** MiRNAs are short RNA molecules (about 22 nucleotides) that modulate gene expression by interfering with the transcription or translation of their target genes. These RNAs play a fundamental role in various biological processes, including development, differentiation, and stress response.

- **Long Non-Coding RNA (lncRNA):** Unlike miRNAs, lncRNAs are longer RNA molecules that are not translated into proteins. They perform a wide range of functions, including transcriptional regulation, chromatin modification, and nuclear organization. Some lncRNAs are known to have roles in diseases such as cancer, making them interesting targets for therapeutic research.

- **Small Molecule RNA Interference (siRNA):** Similar to miRNAs, siRNAs act by silencing genes through RNA interference mechanisms. They are often used in the laboratory to study gene function but also have a natural role in defense against viruses and transposons.

In Summary: The vast world of epigenetic mechanisms extends well beyond the mere DNA sequence, providing an additional layer of gene regulation that can dynamically respond to internal and external signals. The depth and complexity of these mechanisms underscore the importance of finely tuned gene expression regulation in eukaryotic cells. With an increasing understanding of these mechanisms, new opportunities are emerging for precision medicine and gene therapy.

4. Epigenetics and Human Development

The journey of human development, from the uniqueness of a single zygote to the immense complexity of an adult composed of billions of specialized cells, is a wonder of biology. This incredible transformation, where each cell carries the same DNA but exhibits diverse properties and functions, is largely guided by the epigenetic landscape. How epigenetics guides development from embryo to adult:

- **Post-Fertilization Reprogramming:** After fertilization, the embryo undergoes a widespread epigenetic reprogramming. Most DNA methyl marks are removed, preparing the embryo for early divisions and setting the stage for cell fate. This epigenetic reset is crucial to erase germline-specific epigenetic imprints and prepare for embryonic development.

- **Epigenetic Stabilization:** As embryonic development progresses, stable epigenetic patterns begin to form, determining the fate and function of cells. These epigenetic patterns are essential to ensure that, for example, a muscle cell grows and functions as a muscle cell, while a neuron does the same in a neuronal context.

- **Plasticity and Environmental Response:** While epigenetic patterns are largely stable throughout life, they can still change in response to environmental cues. This plasticity allows individuals to adapt to new environments and challenges. For instance, maternal nutrition during pregnancy can influence the fetus's epigenetic profile, with consequences that may persist into adulthood.

Cell Differentiation and Specialization: From Totipotent to Pluripotent: During the early stages of embryo development, cells are totipotent, meaning they have the ability to develop into any type of cell, including embryonic attachments like the placenta. However, as development progresses, these cells lose this unlimited capacity and become pluripotent, capable of becoming any type of body cell but no longer embryonic attachments.

Epigenetic Markers and Cell Fate: During the differentiation process, specific genes are activated or repressed through epigenetic modifications. For example, in differentiation into a muscle cell, specific muscle genes will be demethylated and activated, while other genes will be methylated and silenced.

Epigenetic Memory: Once a cell has reached a specialized state, the "memory" of this state is maintained through epigenetic marks. This ensures that, for example, a skin cell continues to behave like a skin cell, even after multiple cell divisions. Epigenetics is fundamental to human development, guiding the differentiation and specialization of every cell in the body. Through a complex interplay of molecular mechanisms, each cell acquires and maintains a unique identity, allowing the formation and function of different tissues and organs. The importance of epigenetics extends beyond the pure biology of development, with implications in diseases, environmental adaptations, and even evolution.

4. Epigenetics and Human Development: Insights and New Considerations

The role of epigenetics in human development is so central that it continues to be the focus of numerous scientific studies. Going beyond mere cell stabilization and differentiation, we see how epigenetics influences deeper and more complex aspects of human development.

Epigenetic Inheritance: While DNA is the primary vehicle of genetic inheritance, epigenetic changes can also be passed from one generation to the next. This phenomenon, known as epigenetic inheritance, suggests that the environmental experiences of our ancestors can influence our epigenetics and, consequently, our health and development.

Epigenetics and Developmental Disorders: Disorders such as Prader-Willi syndrome or Angelman syndrome are caused by defects in gene imprinting, an epigenetic process. Abnormalities in this mechanism can lead to severe developmental and health problems. Understanding how epigenetics influences these conditions can offer new avenues for treatments or therapies.

Environmental Influence and Critical Periods: There are times in prenatal and infant development, known as "critical windows," when the organism is particularly sensitive to environmental influences. During these phases, factors such as nutrition, stress, or exposure to toxic substances can induce lasting epigenetic changes that affect long-term health.

Epigenetics and the Nervous System: The brain, with its remarkable plasticity and capacity for learning and memory, is deeply influenced by epigenetics. Epigenetic changes in the brain can impact behavior, learning, and memory. Moreover, they have been identified as key factors in neurological and psychiatric conditions such as depression, autism, and schizophrenia.

Adaptation and Evolution: Epigenetics can also play a role in species adaptation to environmental changes. Since epigenetic changes can be rapidly induced in response to the environment, they can provide a mechanism through which populations can adapt to new environments relatively quickly, long before DNA-level changes occur.

Expanded Conclusion: Understanding epigenetics has revolutionized our understanding of development and human biology. It's not just about understanding how a single embryo develops into a complex adult, but also about understanding how experiences, the environment, and even the history of our species can leave an indelible mark on our DNA, influencing present and future generations. Epigenetics lies at the intersection of genetics, developmental biology, neuroscience, medicine, and even anthropology, offering an integrated view of human life and its ongoing evolution.

5. Environmental Factors and Epigenetics

Epigenetics serves as a bridge between genetics and the environment, representing one of the primary avenues through which the environment can influence gene expression and, consequently, the health and behavior of organisms. The relationship between environmental factors and epigenetic changes is complex and deeply intertwined, and understanding it could unveil the mechanisms behind numerous diseases and conditions.

How the Environment Can Influence Epigenetic Changes: Molecular Mechanisms: Cells possess sophisticated signaling networks that enable them to perceive and respond to environmental changes. These signals can activate specific cellular pathways that, in turn, recruit or activate enzymes involved in DNA methylation, histone modification, or non-coding RNA production. This determines whether a specific gene is activated or repressed.

Epigenetic Plasticity: Unlike the DNA sequence, which remains largely static throughout life, an individual's epigenetic landscape can change in response to the environment. This plasticity allows cells and tissues to adapt rapidly to environmental changes but can also lead to lasting epigenetic alterations that influence long-term health.

Examples of External Factors: Diet: Nutrition is one of the most influential environmental factors on epigenetics. Specific nutrients can act as cofactors for enzymes involved in epigenetic modifications. For instance, methionine, an amino acid, is a key source of methyl groups used in DNA methylation. Deficiency or excess of certain nutrients can disrupt normal epigenetic patterns, affecting disease predisposition, metabolism, and tissue function.

Stress: Exposure to stressful situations, both acute and chronic, can induce profound changes in the epigenetic landscape, especially in the brain. These changes can affect the expression of genes involved in stress response, synaptic plasticity, and neuroendocrine functions. Long-term consequences of stress may include increased susceptibility to conditions such as depression, anxiety, and other psychiatric illnesses.

Pollution: Exposure to environmental chemicals, such as heavy metals, industrial chemicals, or air pollutants, can influence epigenetics. For instance, lead exposure in early life has been associated with DNA methylation changes that may persist into adulthood. Pollution can disrupt normal epigenetic regulation mechanisms, leading to diseases like asthma, cardiovascular diseases, and certain types of cancer.

Further Insights: Gene-Environment Interactions: Not all individuals respond to environmental stimuli in the same way. This can be due to genetic variations that influence sensitivity to epigenetic changes. These gene-environment interactions can explain why some people are more susceptible to environmentally induced diseases than others.

Therapeutic Implications: Understanding how the environment influences epigenetics could pave the way for new epigenetic treatments. For example, drugs that modify DNA methylation or histone modification could be used to treat diseases related to epigenetic dysfunctions.

The environment in which we live not only shapes our life experiences but also our biology at the molecular level. The relationship between environmental factors and epigenetics offers a fascinating view of how life and the environment are deeply and intricately interconnected. As we continue to uncover the secrets of this interaction, new possibilities emerge for understanding health, disease, and the nature of human beings.

The Importance of Early Life Experiences: Fetal-Neonatal Epigenetic Programming:
Events during fetal and neonatal development

can have long-term effects on health through epigenetic mechanisms. For example, maternal malnutrition during pregnancy can lead to epigenetic changes in the fetus that increase the risk of metabolic diseases in adulthood.

Early Exposures: Studies have shown that exposure to certain environmental factors in early life, such as nutritional deficiencies, stress, or exposure to toxic substances, can have lasting effects on health through epigenetic mechanisms. This period is particularly sensitive to epigenetic changes because it is when many of the epigenetic marks are first "set."

Interplay between Genetics and Epigenetics: Individual Epigenetic Variation: In addition to genetic differences, there are epigenetic variations among individuals. Some of these epigenetic differences may be inherited, while others may result from unique environmental exposures or life events.

Epigenetics and Chronic Diseases:
Cardiometabolic Diseases: There is growing evidence of the role of epigenetics in cardiometabolic diseases such as diabetes and cardiovascular diseases. Factors like diet, physical activity, and stress can influence the risk of these diseases through epigenetic mechanisms.

Cancer: Some carcinogenic environmental agents can cause epigenetic changes that contribute to tumorigenesis. These changes can lead to the activation of oncogenes or the inactivation of tumor suppressor genes.

Social Environment and Epigenetics:
Socioeconomic Status: Studies suggest that socioeconomic status can influence health through epigenetic mechanisms. Individuals

with lower socioeconomic status may have different epigenetic patterns, potentially due to increased exposure to stressors or suboptimal nutritional intake.

Trauma and Mental Health: Traumas, such as physical or emotional abuse, can leave an "epigenetic imprint," influencing gene expression in ways that increase the risk of conditions like depression, PTSD, and other mental disorders.

Conclusions: The effects of environmental factors on epigenetics represent a complex interplay of genes, the environment, and time. Understanding how these factors combine and interact can offer new insights into the causes of diseases and prevention strategies. Considering that epigenetics can be potentially reversible, it also holds the promise of new treatments and therapeutic interventions for a range of conditions.

Epigenetics and Biological Systems: Immune System: The environment can have a significant impact on the immune system through epigenetic modifications. For example, exposure to pathogens can alter the epigenome of immune cells, such as T and B lymphocytes, influencing their ability to respond to future infections.

Endocrine System: Hormones like cortisol, which increase in response to stress, can also induce epigenetic changes. These changes can have a lasting effect on how the body manages stress and regulates metabolism.

Early Exposure and Long-Term Health:

Prenatal Exposure: Environmental effects can begin in the womb. For example, if a mother is exposed to environmental toxins during pregnancy, it can lead to epigenetic changes in the fetus, with potential long-term effects on the individual's health.

Epigenetic Programming: Exposure to environmental factors during critical developmental stages, such as infancy and adolescence, can "program" the epigenome to influence health and behavior in adulthood.

Ethical and Social Implications:

Epigenetic Inequalities: Environmental effects are not evenly distributed in the population. Individuals in adverse environments or unfavorable socioeconomic conditions are more susceptible to harmful epigenetic changes, contributing to health inequalities.

Privacy Concerns: With the advancement of epigenetic technologies, the issue of privacy of epigenetic data arises, as it could reveal sensitive information about an individual's environmental exposure history.

Other Sources of Epigenetic Variation:

Age: The epigenetic landscape changes with age, and these changes can be accelerated by environmental factors such as diet, stress, and chemical exposure.

Sex: There are also epigenetic differences between males and females, and some of these differences can be influenced by environmental factors, such as sex hormones.

Conclusion: The relationship between environmental factors and epigenetics is fascinating and complex. A deep understanding of it could not only help us treat a range of diseases but also provide insight into how the environment we live in shapes who we are at a very deep and intrinsic level.

6. Epigenetics and Diseases Epigenetics plays a crucial role in gene regulation, so it's not surprising that any disruption in this balance can cause or contribute to various diseases. Some of the epigenetic changes may be due to environmental factors, genetics, or a combination of both.

Cases of Epigenetic Modifications and Diseases:

Prader-Willi Syndrome and Angelman Syndrome: These are classic examples of genetic diseases associated with epigenetic changes. Both syndromes are caused by abnormalities in a specific region of chromosome 15. The difference between the two conditions depends on which parent provided the altered chromosome, highlighting the importance of epigenetics in gene expression regulation.

Neurodegenerative Diseases: Research has shown that diseases like Alzheimer's and Parkinson's may be linked to epigenetic changes. Changes in DNA methylation and histone modifications have been observed in the brains of patients with these diseases.

Psychiatric Disorders: Conditions like depression, schizophrenia, and autism have been associated with epigenetic variations. For example, altered methylation of specific genes can influence synaptic transmission in the brain, affecting brain function and behavior.

Epigenetics and Cancer:

Cancer is perhaps the area where epigenetics has received the most attention. Epigenetic alterations can lead to the activation of oncogenes or the inactivation of tumor suppressor genes, resulting in uncontrolled cell growth.

Silencing of Tumor Suppressor Genes: Many cancers are characterized by the silencing of genes that normally protect against cancer. This silencing can be caused by abnormal DNA methylation, preventing the expression of these vital genes.

Oncogenes: Conversely, some genes that promote cell growth, known as oncogenes, can become overactive due to epigenetic changes. This overexpression can lead to uncontrolled cell proliferation.

Epigenetic Therapies in Cancer: Considering the importance of epigenetics in cancer, it's not surprising that epigenetic therapies have emerged to treat cancer. These drugs aim to "reset" the tumor's epigenome, reactivating tumor suppressor genes or inhibiting oncogenes.

Conclusion: Epigenetics has revolutionized our understanding of diseases. In addition to looking at DNA mutations, scientists now also examine how DNA is regulated. This awareness has led to new treatments and therapies, and with further research, there is hope for developing more effective and personalized cures for a wide range of diseases.

Heart Disease and Methylation: Cardiac Implications: Recent research suggests that epigenetic changes can play a role in the development of heart diseases. Aberrations in

DNA methylation at specific gene sites can influence cardiac function and the progression of conditions like atherosclerosis.

Environment and the Heart: Exposure to environmental risk factors, such as a high-fat diet, can cause epigenetic changes that increase the risk of heart diseases. These changes can persist over time, even if an individual changes their lifestyle.

Epigenetics and Diabetes: Methylation and Insulin: Type 2 diabetes, in particular, has shown associations with epigenetic alterations. Abnormal regulation of genes involved in insulin secretion and action can contribute to the onset of diabetes.

Prenatal Factors: Studies suggest that exposure to malnutrition in utero can cause epigenetic changes in the fetus, increasing the risk of diabetes and other metabolic conditions in adulthood.

Epigenetics and Autoimmune Dysfunctions:
Immune Regulation: Autoimmune diseases like rheumatoid arthritis and systemic lupus erythematosus exhibit distinct epigenetic profiles. Epigenetic dysregulation in these conditions can alter the immune response, causing the body to attack its own tissues.

Environment and Autoimmunity: Exposure to specific environmental factors can trigger epigenetic changes that, in turn, activate or exacerbate autoimmune responses. For example, sunlight exposure in predisposed individuals can induce epigenetic changes that trigger lupus.

Epigenetic Drugs and Personalized Care: **Modifiers of the Epigenome:** New drugs are in development to specifically target abnormal epigenetic changes. For instance, histone deacetylase inhibitors are drugs that can influence the epigenome and are currently under investigation for the treatment of various diseases. **Personalized Therapies:** With the ability to map an individual's epigenome, there is the potential to develop tailored treatments. This personalized approach could enhance treatment efficacy and reduce side effects. In summary, as the relationship between epigenetics and disease continues to emerge and become increasingly clear, what is evident is that epigenetics plays a key role in many pathological conditions. The ability to understand and potentially manipulate the epigenome could open new frontiers in the medicine of the future.

Epigenetic Impact on Cardiovascular Diseases: Dyslipidemia and Atherosclerosis: Studies suggest that epigenetic modifications can influence cholesterol levels and the function of endothelial cells in blood vessels, factors contributing to diseases like atherosclerosis. **Hypertension:** Aberrant methylation of specific genes involved in blood pressure regulation has been observed in animal and human models of hypertension. **Autoimmune Diseases: Rheumatoid Arthritis:** Epigenetic changes in the DNA of immune cells such as T and B lymphocytes have been associated with rheumatoid arthritis. **Lupus:** This is another autoimmune disease where epigenetic modifications have been found, particularly in altering the expression of genes that control the immune response. **Metabolic Diseases: Diabetes:** Epigenetics has been linked to type 2 diabetes through the methylation of genes regulating insulin and glucose homeostasis. **Obesity:** Some studies suggest that obesity may be partially regulated by epigenetic factors, including modifications that affect appetite and lipid metabolism. **Therapy Personalization: Epigenetic Pharmacogenomics:** Some drugs may have varying efficacy depending on the patient's epigenetic status. This emerging field aims to personalize pharmacological therapy based on the patient's epigenetic profile.

Prevention and Prognosis: Epigenetic Biomarkers: Epigenetic changes can serve as biomarkers for early diagnosis or prognosis of various diseases, including cancer.

Preventive Therapies: Understanding epigenetic mechanisms could lead to interventions that prevent the development of diseases by modulating the epigenome. **Conclusion:** The discovery of the crucial role of epigenetics in a wide range of diseases is bringing significant advancements in medicine. It could not only lead to new methods of diagnosis and treatment but also offer avenues for disease prevention in high-risk individuals. The key will be to continue research to understand the precise mechanisms through which epigenetic modifications influence health and disease.

7. Epigenetics and Behavior:

Epigenetics, with its reversible genome modifications, stands at the intersection of genetics and the environment. One of the most fascinating areas of epigenetic research is exploring how epigenetic modifications can influence human behavior. This section will delve into the link between epigenetics and behavior through studies on twins and how these modifications can shape our personality, choices, and behaviors.

Twin Studies and What They Reveal About Epigenetics and Personality: Monozygotic and Dizygotic Twins: Twin studies provide a unique platform to examine epigenetic differences. While monozygotic twins share the same DNA, their epigenetic markers may differ. These differences become particularly evident when one twin develops a condition, such as a disease, while the other does not.

Environmental Factors: Starting from the womb, twins can be exposed to different environmental conditions, leading to variations in their epigenetic markers. For example, prenatal stress or nutritional differences can induce different epigenetic modifications in twins.

Influences on Personality: Some research suggests that differences in DNA methylation may be associated with differences in personality traits such as extraversion or anxiety. Longitudinal studies on twins can reveal whether these differences are stable over time and what their impact on behavior and well-being might be.

How Epigenetics Could Influence Our Choices and Behaviors: Early Experiences: Traumatic events during childhood, such as abuse or neglect, can lead to epigenetic modifications that persist into adulthood. These modifications can influence stress responses, emotional regulation, and even susceptibility to disorders like depression.

Addictions: There is a correlation between substance use and epigenetic modifications. Some drugs, such as cocaine or nicotine, can alter the epigenetic status of specific genes in the brain, thereby influencing addiction-related behaviors.

Diet and Behavior: Diet and nutrition can have an epigenetic effect. For example, a diet rich in processed foods or excessive sugars can induce changes in gene expression that affect behaviors like appetite, satiety, or food-seeking.

Learning and Memory: Epigenetics plays a role in learning and memory. Epigenetic modifications in the brain can influence synaptic plasticity and the formation of new neuronal connections, essential for learning and information retention.

Conclusion: The link between epigenetics and behavior is a rapidly evolving field that offers profound insights into the nature of human behavior. As our understanding deepens, it is likely that new opportunities for therapies and interventions targeting the epigenetic underpinnings of behaviors and behavioral disorders will emerge.

Maternal-Infant Communication and Epigenetic Marks: Mother-Child Connection: During pregnancy, the maternal environment profoundly impacts the fetal epigenetic development. This connection doesn't end at birth. Breastfeeding, for example, can influence the child's epigenetic profile in response to nutrients present in breast milk.

Epigenetic Response to Trauma: A child's response to early traumas, such as separation from the mother or exposure to stressful situations, can induce epigenetic changes that affect long-term mental health. These modifications can predispose the child to issues like anxiety, depression, and behavioral disorders.

Socialization and Relationships: Social Epigenomics: Our interaction with the social environment can influence epigenetic profiles.

Life experiences such as relationships, friendships, and work experiences can induce epigenetic modifications that, in turn, modulate our social behavior and emotional responses.

Isolation and Loneliness: Studies have shown that prolonged isolation and loneliness can lead to specific epigenetic modifications, which may be correlated with conditions like depression and mood disorders.

Epigenetic Factors and Behavioral Responses: Stress Response: Epigenetics plays a role in modulating our stress response. Changes in the epigenetic profile can influence the production and response to stress hormones, affecting our ability to cope with stressful situations.

Brain Reward System: Epigenetic modifications can influence the brain's reward system, which is crucial for sensations like pleasure, happiness, and motivation. These modifications can impact how we react to positive or negative experiences and make decisions.

Final Reflections: The field of epigenetics is opening new frontiers in understanding human behavior. While many connections between epigenetics and behavior are still being explored, it is clear that our DNA is not the sole determinant of who we are and how we act. Epigenetic changes offer a new lens through which we can examine and understand the complex interplay between genes and the environment and how this interaction manifests in our daily behavior.

Memory and Learning:

Epigenetic Changes and Neuroplasticity: The brain's ability to change and adapt is known as neuroplasticity. This plasticity is crucial for learning and memory. Some epigenetic modifications in the brain can either facilitate or inhibit the formation of new synaptic connections, directly influencing the capacity for learning and memory.

Implications for Degenerative Diseases: Alterations in epigenetic mechanisms can lead to memory dysfunctions, which are often observed in neurodegenerative diseases such as Alzheimer's.

Addictive Behavior: Addiction and Epigenetic Changes: Substances like alcohol, nicotine, and drugs can cause epigenetic changes in the brain. These changes can affect susceptibility to addiction, the intensity of addiction, and the ability to abstain from further consumption. **Future Treatments:** Understanding these epigenetic changes could lead to the development of new treatments for addictions by directly targeting epigenetic modulation.

Impulsivity and Aggression:

Epigenetic Mechanisms in Aggression: Some studies suggest that epigenetic modifications may play a role in regulating aggression and impulsivity. For example, altered methylation of specific genes may lead to more aggressive behaviors in certain individuals.

Implications for Therapy: This understanding could offer new therapeutic perspectives for behavioral disorders by focusing on epigenetic modulation to reduce aggression and impulsivity.

Epigenetics and Chronobiology: Circadian Rhythms: Our behavioral responses to day-night cycles are partly regulated by epigenetic mechanisms. Epigenetic changes can influence our internal biological clock, regulating circadian rhythms and affecting behaviors such as sleep, eating, and mood.

Conclusion: Epigenetics, being at the intersection of genetics and the environment, has a profound impact on many facets of human behavior. Its understanding can offer a more comprehensive view of how our genes, experiences, and the environment collectively shape who we are. As research in this field expands, it will be possible to develop more effective strategies for the prevention and treatment of numerous behavioral and neurological disorders.

8. Epigenetic Manipulation and Its Implications: Epigenetic manipulation represents one of the most promising but also controversial areas of modern molecular biology. It has opened new possibilities in the field of medicine, but with these opportunities come a series of ethical challenges and risks.

The Possibility of "Editing" Epigenetic Modifications: Epigenetic Drugs: Recently, drugs that can influence epigenetics have been developed, such as histone deacetylase inhibitors (HDACs) and DNA demethylating agents. These drugs are under investigation for a variety of applications, particularly in the field of oncology. **Editing Technologies:** Some technological advancements, like CRISPR, not only allow for DNA editing but can also be used to induce specific epigenetic modifications. This could offer much more precise control over gene regulation without altering the DNA sequence itself.

Cell Reprogramming: The ability to reprogram cells (e.g., converting a differentiated cell into a pluripotent stem cell) is partly based on rewriting the cell's epigenetic profile. This has significant implications for regenerative medicine.

Ethical Considerations and Potential Risks:

Epigenetic Therapies: While therapies that modify an individual's epigenetic profile may offer solutions to previously incurable diseases, there is a risk that these modifications may not be permanent or may influence non-target genes, causing unforeseen side effects. **Germline Manipulation:** If epigenetic modifications are made to germ cells (sperm or eggs), these changes could be passed on to future generations. This raises significant ethical questions as future generations have no say in these modifications. **Human "Enhancement":** The idea of using epigenetic manipulation not only to treat diseases but also to "enhance" human abilities (e.g., intelligence, longevity, physical endurance) opens an ethical debate. Where is the line drawn between therapy and enhancement? **Accessibility and Inequality:**

There is a potential risk that these advanced technologies will only be accessible to the wealthy, creating further inequality in society. Who should have access to these technologies, and at what cost?

Environmental Implications: Epigenetic interventions could have unknown effects on the environment, especially if used in organisms like plants or animals that can interact with larger ecosystems.

In-Depth on Epigenetic Manipulation:

Maturation of Epigenetic Therapies: While epigenetic therapies have shown initial promise, their maturation as standard treatments requires further research. For example, while some epigenetic therapies have demonstrated efficacy in the laboratory, not all have shown the same success in clinical trials. Reasons may include differences in the tumor microenvironment and the patient's immune system. **Precision and Specificity:** A significant hurdle for epigenetic manipulation is its specificity. While CRISPR has revolutionized genetic editing for its precision, epigenetic manipulation, such as with HDAC inhibitors, can affect multiple genes and cellular pathways. The challenge is to develop tools that can target specific epigenetic sites with minimal error.

Psychological Implications: Epigenetic manipulation, especially when it comes to behavioral or psychological traits, can have profound psychological implications. For example, if a person were to know that a certain aspect of their behavior or personality could be "altered" through epigenetic interventions, this could raise questions about identity, agency, and personal responsibility.

Informed Consent Issues: Since epigenetic manipulation is a relatively new field, there may be unknown long-term effects. This raises issues of informed consent, especially if patients are adequately informed about potential risks and benefits.

Real-World Ethical Dilemmas: Imagine a world where companies offer "epigenetic optimization" services to enhance intelligence or other abilities. This raises issues of authenticity, justice (who can afford these treatments?), and even cultural evolution (how would society change if such services became commonplace?).

Implications for Longevity and Aging: Epigenetic manipulation has also shown potential in the field of aging. If we could "reset" the epigenetic profile of our cells, could we possibly slow down the aging process? This not only opens new frontiers in longevity research but also raises ethical questions about human lifespan and the social implications of extended life.

These are just some of the many aspects related to epigenetic manipulation and its implications. It is a rapidly evolving field and will undoubtedly continue to offer new discoveries and challenges.

Long-Term Effects and Longitudinal Studies:

Long-Term Effects of Modifications: One of the most serious concerns is the long-term effects of induced epigenetic modifications. While some of these modifications may seem beneficial in the short term, it is unclear how they might affect the organism in the long term or even across different generations.

Longitudinal Studies: To better understand long-term effects, longitudinal studies tracking individuals over time are needed. However, these studies can be costly, time-consuming, and present ethical challenges.

Regulation and Legislation:

Need for Guidelines: Currently, the regulation of epigenetic manipulation is a gray area. International guidelines are needed to govern the ethical use of these technologies.

Legislative Process: Creating laws that regulate the use of epigenetic manipulation could be a lengthy and complex process, with numerous stakeholders involved, from scientists and medical professionals to legislators and civil rights activists.

Commercial Applications and Patents:

Intellectual Property: The implications of intellectual property and patents related to epigenetic technologies are enormous. Who owns the rights to a particular epigenetic modification? What if this modification is passed on to future generations?

Market and Commercialization: With the advent of effective epigenetic therapies, there will inevitably be a market for these. How will the price of such treatments be determined? And what kind of access will low-income patients have?

Social Responsibility and Public Perception:

Public Perception: The acceptance of such powerful technologies is closely linked to their public perception. Misinformation campaigns or accidents could slow down or hinder progress in the field.

Social Responsibility: Scientists and industry professionals have a social responsibility to ensure that technologies are used responsibly.

Public education and transparency in research are crucial in this context.

These are just some of the many aspects that may be considered when discussing epigenetic manipulation and its implications.

8. Epigenetic Manipulation and Its Implications (Extension)

Potential Benefits of Epigenetic Manipulation:

Gene Expression Restoration: Through the use of agents that modify epigenetics, it is possible to restore the expression of genes that have been abnormally silenced, as can occur in many diseases. **Disease Prevention:** Knowledge of epigenetic markers could help identify individuals at risk of developing particular diseases, enabling preventive interventions. **Personalized Therapies:** With an understanding of epigenetic profiles, doctors may one day prescribe personalized treatments based on an individual's specific epigenetic modifications.

Technical Concerns:

Reversibility: Many epigenetic modifications are reversible, meaning that even after a modification intervention, they could revert to their original state. This instability could reduce the effectiveness of some therapies.

Specificity: Ensuring that an epigenetic intervention acts only on the target gene or pathway is a challenge. Unintended modifications to other genes could have severe side effects.

Predictability: While we know that certain epigenetic modifications are associated with specific outcomes, our understanding of the entire epigenetic system is still limited. We cannot always predict precisely how a modification in one part of the system will influence the rest.

Extended Ethical Dilemmas:

Preservation of Identity: If it became possible to modify behavioral or cognitive traits through epigenetic manipulation, it would raise questions about personal identity. To what extent does a person remain "themselves" if such traits are altered?

Informed Consent: For experimental epigenetic therapies, ensuring adequate informed consent could be complicated, as patients may not fully understand the long-term implications or associated risks.

In Utero Modifications: The ability to intervene epigenetically before birth presents unique dilemmas. While it could offer the possibility of preventing diseases, it could also open the door to "designing" children with desired traits, with profound social and moral implications.

Extended Conclusion: Epigenetic manipulation is truly a double-edged sword: it offers the hope of revolutionary cures but brings with it profound ethical, technical, and moral questions. As a society, we must carefully weigh the potential benefits against the risks, ensuring that decisions are made with deep ethical reflection and adequate scientific understanding.

9. Case Studies and Recent Published Research

Epigenetics is one of the most dynamic research areas in biology. In recent years, numerous studies have shed light on the complex mechanisms through which epigenetic modifications influence health, development, and behavior. Here are some noteworthy case studies and research:

1. Effects of Famines on Offspring One of the most famous epigenetic case studies concerns the effect of the Dutch famine of 1944-1945. During this period, many people were exposed to extreme food shortages. Studies have shown that children born to mothers who were pregnant during the famine had a high likelihood of experiencing health issues such as obesity and type 2 diabetes. Years of research have demonstrated that these consequences result from epigenetic modifications induced by malnutrition.

2. Epigenetics and Learning/Memory Recent research has explored how epigenetic modifications in the brain influence learning and memory. It has been discovered, for example, that histone modifications can affect the formation of new memories and neural plasticity. These findings could have implications for the treatment of cognitive or neurodegenerative disorders.

3. Cancer and Epigenetic Changes Numerous studies have linked epigenetic modifications to cancer. For instance, abnormal DNA methylation can silence genes that normally protect against tumor formation. Understanding how these modifications promote cancer development could lead to new therapeutic strategies.

4. Impact of Endocrine Disruptors Recent research has investigated how certain chemical compounds, known as endocrine disruptors, may cause epigenetic modifications. These substances can interfere with the endocrine system and potentially have serious health effects. Investigations are underway into how these substances influence the epigenome and what the long-term consequences might be.

5. CRISPR Technology and Epigenetics

Although CRISPR technology is more commonly associated with direct gene editing, it has recently been adapted to introduce specific epigenetic modifications without altering the underlying DNA sequence. This offers the promise of targeted epigenetic therapies with unprecedented precision.

8. Epigenetic Manipulation and Its Implications (Extension)

Potential Benefits of Epigenetic Manipulation:

Gene Expression Restoration: Through the use of agents that modify epigenetics, it is possible to restore the expression of genes that have been abnormally silenced, as can occur in many diseases. **Disease Prevention:**

Knowledge of epigenetic markers could help identify individuals at risk of developing particular diseases, enabling preventive interventions. **Personalized Therapies:** With an understanding of epigenetic profiles, doctors may one day prescribe personalized treatments based on an individual's specific epigenetic modifications.

Technical Concerns:

Reversibility: Many epigenetic modifications are reversible, meaning that even after a modification intervention, they could revert to their original state. This instability could reduce the effectiveness of some therapies.

Specificity: Ensuring that an epigenetic intervention acts only on the target gene or pathway is a challenge. Unintended modifications to other genes could have severe side effects. **Predictability:** While we know that certain epigenetic modifications are associated with specific outcomes, our understanding of the entire epigenetic system is still limited. We cannot always predict precisely how a modification in one part of the system will influence the rest.

Extended Ethical Dilemmas:

Preservation of Identity: If it became possible to modify behavioral or cognitive traits through epigenetic manipulation, it would raise questions about personal identity. To what extent does a person remain "themselves" if such traits are altered?

Informed Consent: For experimental epigenetic therapies, ensuring adequate informed consent could be complicated, as patients may not fully understand the long-term implications or associated risks.

In Utero Modifications: The ability to intervene epigenetically before birth presents unique dilemmas. While it could offer the possibility of preventing diseases, it could also open the door to "designing" children with desired traits, with profound social and moral implications.

Extended Conclusion: Epigenetic manipulation is truly a double-edged sword: it offers the hope of revolutionary cures but brings with it profound ethical, technical, and moral questions. As a society, we must carefully weigh the potential benefits against the risks, ensuring that decisions are made with deep ethical reflection and adequate scientific understanding.

9. Case Studies and Recent Published Research

Epigenetics is one of the most dynamic research areas in biology. In recent years, numerous studies have shed light on the complex mechanisms through which epigenetic modifications influence health, development, and behavior. Here are some noteworthy case studies and research:

1. Effects of Famines on Offspring One of the most famous epigenetic case studies concerns the effect of the Dutch famine of 1944-1945. During this period, many people were exposed to extreme food shortages. Studies have shown that children born to mothers who were pregnant during the famine had a high likelihood of experiencing health issues such as obesity and type 2 diabetes. Years of research have demonstrated that these consequences result from epigenetic modifications induced by malnutrition.

2. Epigenetics and Learning/Memory Recent research has explored how epigenetic modifications in the brain influence learning and memory. It has been discovered, for example, that histone modifications can affect the formation of new memories and neural plasticity. These findings could have implications for the treatment of cognitive or neurodegenerative disorders.

3. Cancer and Epigenetic Changes Numerous studies have linked epigenetic modifications to cancer. For instance, abnormal DNA methylation can silence genes that normally protect against tumor formation. Understanding how these modifications promote cancer development could lead to new therapeutic strategies.

4. Impact of Endocrine Disruptors Recent research has investigated how certain chemical compounds, known as endocrine disruptors, may cause epigenetic modifications. These substances can interfere with the endocrine system and potentially have serious health effects. Investigations are underway into how these substances influence the epigenome and what the long-term consequences might be.

5. CRISPR Technology and Epigenetics Although CRISPR technology is more commonly associated with direct gene editing, it has recently been adapted to introduce specific epigenetic modifications without altering the underlying DNA sequence. This offers the promise of targeted epigenetic therapies with unprecedented precision.

In Conclusion, Epigenetics is an emerging field of study with enormous potential in medicine, biology, and society. Its interaction with other scientific, technological, and social disciplines will ensure it remains at the forefront of science and medicine in the near future.

Prevention through Epigenetics

One particularly interesting aspect is how epigenetics could be used in preventive medicine. If we can identify early epigenetic changes associated with specific diseases, we could intervene before symptoms manifest:

Epigenetic Monitoring: Similar to regular check-ups, we could have epigenetic screenings to identify marks associated with specific diseases and assess individual risk.
Diet and Epigenetics: Diet is one of the most

influential environmental factors on epigenetic modifications. Understanding how specific foods or nutrients influence the epigenetic profile could guide personalized dietary recommendations for disease prevention or maintaining optimal health.

Epigenetics and Aging

Aging is accompanied by a series of epigenetic changes. Understanding and intervening in these modifications could offer new perspectives on extending lifespan and the quality of aging:

Longevity: If epigenetic changes play a role in longevity, strategies could be developed to "reset" the epigenetic clock and delay aging.
Neurodegenerative Diseases: Diseases like Alzheimer's show a connection to epigenetic

changes. Deeper understanding could lead to new treatments or preventive interventions.

Ethics of Epigenetics

As we deepen our understanding and ability to manipulate the epigenetic profile, ethical questions arise:

Programmable Epigenetic Changes: If we became capable of programming epigenetic modifications, what would be the guidelines for what is ethically acceptable? **Access to Information:** Who would have access to an individual's epigenetic data? How might this information be used, for example, by insurance companies or employers? **Public Awareness:** There is a need to educate the public about what epigenetics is and its implications, to enable informed decisions at both individual and societal levels.

Epigenetics, with its tremendous potential, promises to revolutionize our understanding of biology. But as with every great discovery, it brings both opportunities and challenges. The key will be balancing our curiosity and desire for innovation with prudence and consideration for long-term implications.

Impact on Mental Health

Future studies may focus on how epigenetic modifications contribute to mental disorders like depression and anxiety. This could pave the way for targeted therapies that address not only symptoms but also the underlying epigenetic causes.

Bioethics and Social Issues

The ability to manipulate epigenetic marks raises significant ethical questions. For instance, if it were possible to "enhance" intelligence or other traits through epigenetic manipulation, this could create even deeper social inequalities. Public policies will need to address these ethical issues.

Implications for Agriculture and Food

Epigenetics is not just about human health; it also has implications for agriculture. Understanding how environments influence plants at the epigenetic level could lead to more resilient and productive crops.

Epigenetics and Aging

Age is a factor that alters our epigenetic profile. A deeper understanding of how epigenetics is related to aging could provide insights into slowing down or even reversing some aspects of the aging process.

Epigenetics and Biological Clocks

Epigenetic regulation is fundamental to our circadian rhythms and other biological clocks. Better understanding this connection could have implications for everything from sleep to body weight regulation.

Interdisciplinary Dialogue

Epigenetics sits at the intersection of genetics, developmental biology, medicine, and psychology. With the advent of big data and artificial intelligence technologies, computer science will also become increasingly important for analyzing epigenetic data.

Implications in Forensic Medicine

As science progresses, an individual's epigenetic profile could one day be used in forensic investigations, providing another layer of information beyond DNA alone.

Personalization of Medicine

Epigenetics has the potential to revolutionize personalized medicine. Once we have a deeper understanding of individual epigenetic changes, doctors may be able to recommend specific treatments based on the patient's epigenetic profile rather than adopting a "one-size-fits-all" approach.

Environment and Climate Change

The epigenetic response to environmental stresses will be crucial in understanding how species, including humans, will adapt to the rapid climate changes underway. This could help develop strategies to conserve at-risk species and assist human communities in facing the challenges of climate change.

Prenatal and Childhood Epigenetics

Environmental influences experienced by a mother during pregnancy can have epigenetic effects on the fetus. Understanding these changes could lead to specific dietary and behavioral recommendations for pregnant women, aimed at optimizing the child's epigenetic health.

New Tools and Techniques

Advancements in technologies such as high-resolution DNA sequencing and big data analysis will offer new opportunities to explore the epigenome with unprecedented precision. This could lead to the discovery of new epigenetic mechanisms and an understanding of how they interact with each other.

Implications in Cancer Treatment

Some forms of cancer originate from epigenetic abnormalities. The future may see the development of anti-cancer therapies that specifically target and correct these abnormalities, offering more targeted treatments with fewer side effects.

Education and Public Awareness

As epigenetics becomes increasingly relevant to our health and well-being, it will be essential to educate the public about what it truly means and how it can influence our daily lives. This could lead to changes in public health policies and dietary recommendations.

International Collaborations

Given the broad scope of epigenetics and its global relevance, we are likely to see increased collaboration among researchers from different countries. These joint efforts could accelerate discoveries and their practical applications.

In summary, epigenetics is a rapidly evolving frontier that promises to bring profound transformations in numerous sectors of science, medicine, and society as a whole.

Conclusion

Epigenetics has emerged as one of the most exciting and dynamic frontiers in biomedical science. This discipline has not only revealed how genes interact with the environment to shape our biology but has also offered a new understanding of the very nature of inheritance and evolution.

Throughout the course of this book, we have explored the underlying mechanisms of epigenetics, its interaction with various aspects of human development, and how the environment and external factors can influence epigenetic modifications. We have also examined epigenetics in relation to diseases, behavior, and potential therapeutic applications.

In an era where our society is increasingly influenced by environmental factors, from pollution to modern diets, and chronic stress, understanding epigenetics becomes even more crucial. It can provide us with the tools to decipher the intricate interplay between genes and the environment and to develop targeted interventions to promote health and prevent diseases.

However, with the growing ability to manipulate epigenetic modifications, new ethical challenges also arise. These technologies promise revolutionary benefits but raise fundamental questions about their safety and long-term implications.

Looking to the future, epigenetics has the potential to revolutionize our approach to medicine, agriculture, and biology in general. However, as with any new scientific frontier, it is essential to proceed with caution, ensuring that new discoveries are used responsibly and for the greater good.

Ultimately, epigenetics reminds us of how intertwined nature and nurture are, and how deep and complex the tapestry of life is. It invites reflection, appreciation for the complexity of life, and the ongoing quest for knowledge. As readers and curious individuals, we have the opportunity and responsibility to stay informed and actively participate in these discussions, shaping a future where science and ethics walk hand in hand.

Milton Keynes UK
Ingram Content Group UK Ltd.
UKHW020732161023
430697UK00016B/752